P9-CDG-709

OCT -- 2018

EXPERIMENT

ATOM

Made by Maxine

written by
Ruth Spiro

illustrated by
Holly Hatam

Dial Books for Young Readers

Think like
a proton.
Always
positive.

For Lily, and all the furry, fuzzy, feathered,
and scaly family members who make our
hearts and homes happier.
-R.S.

Dedicated to the four smartest girls I know;
Jill, Hannah, Mia, and Abigail. Always remember,
you can change the world. xox
-H.H.

Dial Books for Young Readers
Penguin Young Readers Group
An imprint of Penguin Random House LLC
375 Hudson Street
New York, NY 10014

Text copyright © 2018 by Ruth Spiro
Illustrations copyright © 2018 by Holly Hatam

Library of Congress Cataloging-in-Publication Data

Names: Spiro, Ruth, author. | Hatam, Holly, illustrator.
Title: Made by Maxine / Ruth Spiro ; illustrated by Holly Hatam.
Description: New York, NY : Dial Books for Young Readers, [2018] | Summary:
When Maxine's school puts on a pet parade, she creates a unique
contraption to allow her very special pet fish, Milton, to participate.
Identifiers: LCCN 2016044194 | ISBN 9780399186295 (hardcover)
Subjects: | CYAC: Inventors—Fiction. | Parades—Fiction. | Aquarium
fishes—Fiction. | Fishes—Fiction. | Aquariums—Fiction.
Classification: LCC PZ7.S7574 Mad 2018 | DDC [E]—dc23 LC record available at
https://lccn.loc.gov/2016044194

Printed in China
1 3 5 7 9 10 8 6 4 2

Design by Mina Chung • Text set in Napoleone Slab

Meet Maxine.
She likes making new things . . . from old things.

She de-constructs and re-constructs.
Unscrews and re-glues.

Maxine makes everything better.

(Mostly.)

Meet Milton.

From the day Maxine spotted him in the pet shop window, she was hooked. His scales shimmered, his fins fluttered . . . Was he waving to her?

Since he was a fish, it was hard to tell.

Maxine fell in love with Milton.

He was a special fish, and deserved a better home than a boring glass bowl.
"If I can dream it, I can make it!" she said.

And then, she did.
First, she tinkered with some old toys

and made a spectacular tank.

Next, she repurposed a broken bike and made . . .

a pedal-powered fish-feeder.

For a final touch, Maxine repurposed some
vegetables and made . . .

music!

Catchy tune!

Being a fish, he was not much of a dancer.
But Milton wiggled his fins to the beat,
practicing his slick moves.

One day at school, Miss McMiller made an exciting announcement.

"This week we'll have a class Pet Parade!" she said. "We'll meet on the playground after school and then march around the building. If you don't have a pet at home, you may borrow one from our classroom."

"I'll bring Milton, my goldfish!"
said Maxine.

"Milton is a very special fish," she replied.
"You'll see."

At home, Maxine told Milton about the Pet Parade. He bubbled with excitement. Being a fish, he didn't get out much.

"It's okay if you don't have feet," Maxine said. "Fins are perfectly fine. No, they're better than fine. They're fabulous!"

But Milton's
spectacular tank was
also spectacularly heavy.

Maxine moved Milton into his old bowl.
It was boring, but easier to carry.
"This is only temporary," she reassured him.
Then they practiced marching.

SPLISH!

Surf's up!

SPLOSH!

SPLISH!

I feel seasick.

Maxine's enthusiasm was dampened,
along with her sneakers.

"We need to make this bowl better," said Maxine.

She collected containers from all around the house.

Maxine fitted and filled,

fixed and fiddled,

. . . and failed.

"Maybe this isn't such a good idea. Maybe I should borrow the class hamster, instead."

Was Milton crying? Since he was a fish, it was hard to tell.

As the big day approached, the Pet Parade was all anyone could talk about.

Maxine thought about Milton, with his shimmering scales and fluttery fins. He was beautiful and funny and smart and talented and . . .

He was her friend.

Sorry, hamster.
I'm marching with Milton.

After school, Maxine picked up her pencils and paper, and planned her project.

She had already discovered a million ways that would not work. Which meant she was getting closer to finding a way that would.

She repurposed a race car,

upcycled an umbrella,

and reprogrammed an old remote.

All afternoon she de-constructed and re-constructed,

unscrewed and re-glued.

She tinkered and hacked,

bent parts forward and back.

Maxine made a

music-playing,

fin-wiggling,

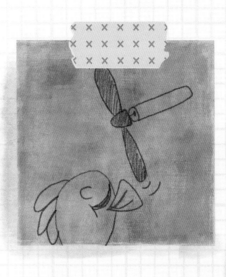

wave-sensing,

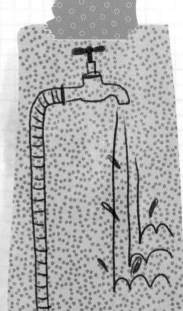

wheel-spinning,

dance-powered...

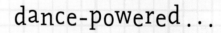
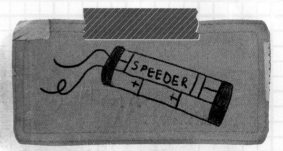

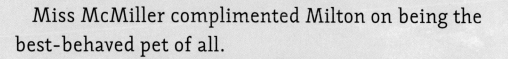

Miss McMiller complimented Milton on being the best-behaved pet of all.

Was he blushing? Since he was a fish, it was hard to tell. She also complimented Maxine on finding a way to include Milton.

"If I can dream it, I can make it!" Maxine said.